W9-AFE-749

THE
EMPRESS
AND THE
SILKWORM

Lily Toy Hong

Albert Whitman & Company · Morton Grove, Illinois

Text and illustrations copyright © 1995
by Lily Toy Hong.
Published in 1995 by Albert Whitman & Company,
6340 Oakton Street, Morton Grove, Illinois 60053.
Published simultaneously in Canada
by General Publishing, Limited, Toronto.
Printed in the U.S.A.
10 9 8 7 6 5 4 3 2 1

The illustrations were done in airbrushed acrylics
and gouache.
The text typeface is Stone Informal.
Designed by Karen Johnson Campbell.

Library of Congress Cataloging-in-Publication Data
Hong, Lily Toy.
The empress and the silkworm / written and illustrated by
Lily Toy Hong.
     p.   cm.
Summary: A fictionalized account of the empress of
China's discovery, around 2700 B.C., that the cocoons of
the worms in her mulberry trees were made of fine, shiny,
silken thread which could be made into beautiful cloth.
ISBN 0-8075-2009-8
[1. Silk—Fiction. 2. China—Fiction.] I. Title.
PZ7.H7475Em 1995   94-49612
[E]—dc20   CIP
                                                 AC

LILY TOY HONG grew up in a large Chinese-American family, the seventh of nine children. She says she always knew she wanted to write and illustrate children's books.

Ms. Hong is also the author and illustrator of *How the Ox Star Fell from Heaven* and *Two of Everything*.

For my boys,
Evan and Elliot, with love.

Nearly five thousand years ago, Huang-Ti, known as the Yellow Emperor, ruled the ancient land of China. He and his young wife, Si Ling-Chi, lived in an enormous palace with a

golden roof. Its pillars were carved with the image of the mighty dragon, symbol of the emperor's strength. Around the palace were gardens and a vast grove of mulberry trees.

The empress loved to stroll through the gardens each morning. From time to time, she caught a glimpse of the phoenix resting upon the palace roof. Everyone knew that to see this bird was a blessing, a sign of good fortune.

On one such lucky morning, Si Ling-Chi was enjoying the shade of the mulberry trees when her maidservant arrived, carrying a tray of delicious mooncakes and hot tea. "Tea time!" she sang as she placed the tray at Si Ling-Chi's feet.

"Oh, they smell so sweet," said the empress. "I can't wait to taste one." She picked up a cake, but as she reached for her teacup—plop! Something splashed right into it.

"Ai-ya!" screamed the maidservant, wrinkling her nose in disgust.

"What is it?" asked Si Ling-Chi.

"I don't know," said the maidservant, shuddering. "I will bring you a fresh cup."

"No, wait," the empress said. She leaned forward to examine the tea. Her eyes grew large with excitement as she saw what was floating on top. It was small and round and white. It was a cocoon! She had seen the tiny worms in the mulberry trees spin these tight blankets around themselves.

In the hot tea, the cocoon was beginning to unwind. She took it out and pulled the loose end gently. The cocoon seemed to be made of a fine, shiny thread.

"Please, Your Highness," the maidservant begged. "Leave that wormy thing alone!"

The empress did not reply, but began to uncoil the strand.

"Look!" she said. "This thread is so light it's almost invisible. It is like a thread fallen from heaven! Come help me unravel it."

From morning to evening, the two unwound the cocoon. They were careful not to break the thread or make a hopeless tangle.

At last they reached the end.

Si Ling-Chi held the silvery thread up in the moonlight. "See how it glistens!" she exclaimed. "But it is so delicate. If we had more strands, we could twist them together to make one thick thread. Go! Bring other servants to help us!"

So through the night Si Ling-Chi and the servants worked, plucking cocoons from the mulberry trees, soaking them in hot tea, and unwinding them. Then they joined all the strands into a single fiber.

The moon hung low in the sky when Si Ling-Chi, exhausted, lay down to rest. While she slept, she had a wonderful dream. She saw the fiery dragon and the proud phoenix rising like the sun. She saw her husband standing among the clouds. He was dressed in a shimmering yellow robe that flowed like the rivers of heaven. The cloth was so beautiful that she knew it could only have been woven from the shining thread of the mulberry cocoons.

When she woke, she knew exactly what she was going to do.

At noon, there was great excitement at the palace. The ladies of the court had formed a procession a mile long. Each gently held part of the miraculous thread. It took a thousand women just to keep it from touching the ground.

A gong was struck. One by one, the ladies of the court entered the room where the emperor sat, surrounded by his advisers. The women paraded the empress's treasure before the throne.

Then Si Ling-Chi approached, holding a tray. Upon it were a caterpillar, a mulberry leaf, a cocoon, and a cup of hot tea.

"What are these things?" asked the emperor. "And what are your servants carrying?"

"I will show you, most honorable husband," she replied.

As the emperor and his advisers watched, she dipped the cocoon into the hot tea.

The advisers began to laugh.

"And this makes the tea taste better, Your Highness?" observed the one with the round belly.

Another joked, "Perhaps it makes the caterpillar taste better!"

Slowly, the empress began to draw the lustrous strand from the cocoon. A hush fell over the court as the strand grew longer. Then Si Ling-Chi told the story of her discovery.

An adviser with a long beard inspected the tiny worm. "Who could imagine," he said, "that something so great could come from something so small!"

"Ah, look how the thread shimmers in the light!" exclaimed another.

"It is as fine as smoke, yet strong as bronze!" cried a third.

Then the round-bellied one said, "Yes, this is truly wonderful, but why should we concern ourselves with it?"

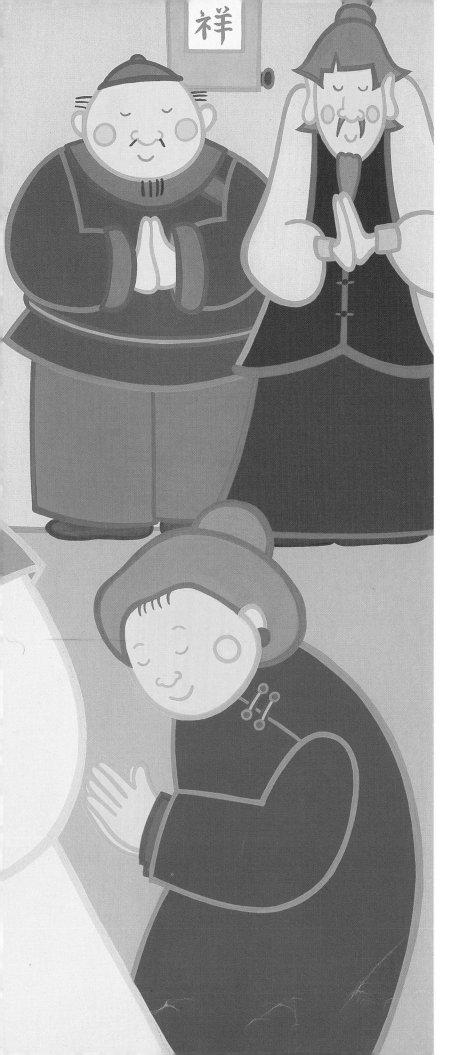

The empress told her dream—how she had seen the Yellow Emperor clothed in a robe woven from the heavenly thread.

For a moment there was silence. Then Huang-Ti smiled at his wife and said, "What a splendid idea! We shall weave a cloth more beautiful than the world has ever seen! Because of this treasure, our kingdom shall be as heaven on earth. I command that none outside this land be told the secret of this noble worm and its precious gift."

With the rising sun, Si Ling-Chi went to work overseeing
the production of the cloth. Imperial gardeners planted more
groves of mulberry trees. Young worms were placed on trays.

Each day fresh leaves were picked and cut to feed them. Royal craftsmen made reels to unwind the cocoons and combine the strands. They built looms to weave the thread into fabric.

Many full moons passed before the

young empress saw the fruits of her labor.

At last, on the morning of the Autumn Moon Festival, a crowd gathered in front of the palace. The great gong sounded, and the red lacquer doors burst open. The people gasped as Huang-Ti stepped out into the light. Wrapped in a billowing robe of radiant yellow, he shone like the sun. It was just as the empress had dreamed.

From that day, the
fabric was called silk. Soon
Si Ling-Chi was known
throughout the kingdom as
the Lady of the Silkworm.

The origin of the
heavenly cloth became one
of the greatest secrets of all
time. For almost three
thousand years, only the
Chinese knew about the
little worm that fed on
mulberry leaves and spun
the beautiful, magical
threads of silk.

According to legend, Huang-Ti, the Yellow Emperor, ruled China from 2697 to 2597 B.C. Legend credits his wife, Empress Si Ling-Chi, with the discovery of silk around 2640 B.C. Some say she also invented the silk reel and the silk loom.

Silk was a rare and precious product. The Chinese did all they could to keep its manufacture a secret. Anyone found carrying silkworm eggs or mulberry tree seeds out of China was punished by death. Westerners greatly desired the rich cloth, and trade was made along the "silk road," a route from China to Damascus (now Syria). But the traders did not learn the secret, either. For nearly three thousand years, no one but the Chinese knew how silk was made.

The secret reached Japan by 3 A.D. Not long after, a Chinese princess hid silkworm eggs in the lining of her headdress when she left her country to marry an Indian prince. In 550 A.D., the Roman emperor, Justinian, sent two spies into China. They returned with silkworm eggs and mulberry seeds in hollow bamboo canes. After that the secret of silk spread across the world.

The silkworm, *Bombyx mori*, is cultivated to produce the finest, whitest silk. First, eggs are laid by the adult moth. They hatch into silkworms and begin to feed on fresh mulberry leaves. After several weeks the silkworm spins its cocoon. At this stage the biggest cocoons are saved for future egg production. The remaining ones are put into hot ovens or dry steamed to kill the silkworm, now called a pupa. Thus, it cannot mature into a moth and burst through the cocoon, damaging the silk.

Then the cocoons are put into boiling water to soften the gum that binds the strands together. The strands become unstuck and can be gently pulled from the cocoon in a single long thread. Because the thread is so fine, five to twelve cocoons are unwound together on a reel to make one stronger thread. These threads are then twisted with others to create a thicker, stronger yarn. Finally the silken yarns are woven into cloth. Dyeing can take place in the yarn or in the cloth.

An average cocoon is one and one-half inches long. Some bigger cocoons have been found to contain a thread one mile long. It takes two to three thousand cocoons to produce one pound of silk fiber. To make ten silk blouses, eight thousand worms have to eat three hundred fifty pounds of mulberry leaves!

JPICT   Hong, Lily Toy.

        The Empress and the
        silkworm.

$16.95

DATE			